AUTHOR DAY

Look for these
and other books
in
The Kids in Ms. Colman's Class series

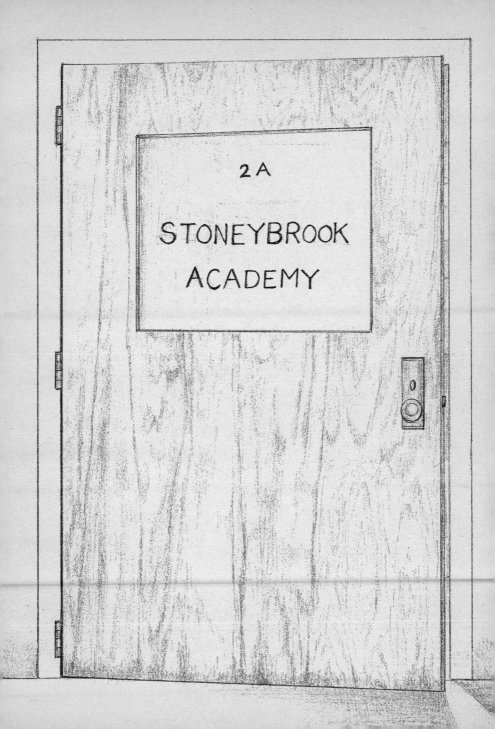

Jannie, Bobby, Tammy, Sara
Ian, Leslie, Hank, Terri
Nancy, Omar, Audrey, Chris, Ms. Colman
Karen, Hannie, Ricky, Natalie

THE KIDS IN Ms. COLMAN'S CLASS

AUTHOR DAY

Ann M. Martin

Illustrations by Charles Tang

A
LITTLE APPLE
PAPERBACK

SCHOLASTIC INC.
New York Toronto London Auckland Sydney

This book is in honor of
Jane Martin and Doug McGrath,
my sister and my brand-new brother-in-law.
Congratulations!

No part of this publication may be reproduced in whole or in part, or stored in a retrieval system, or transmitted in any form or by any means, electronic, mechanical, photocopying, recording, or otherwise, without written permission of the publisher. For information regarding permission, write to Scholastic Inc., 555 Broadway, New York, NY 10012.

ISBN 0-590-26216-5

12 11 10 9 8 7 6 5 4 3 2   6 7 8 9/9 0 1/0

Printed in the U.S.A.   40

First Scholastic printing, March 1996

THE RAINY DAY

Drip, drip, drip. Drip-drop, drip.

Ricky Torres looked out the window of his classroom. He was *trying* to pay attention. But this was hard. It was a rainy, rainy day. The wind was blowing. The trees were swaying. Maybe this was not an ordinary storm. Maybe it was a hurricane. Maybe —

"Ricky? . . . Ricky?"

Ricky blinked. "What?"

"Pay attention!" whispered Hannie Papadakis, who sat next to him.

Ricky looked at his teacher. Ms. Colman was standing patiently at the front of her second-grade classroom. Ms. Colman was almost always patient. And friendly.

1

She was not a yeller. She listened to kids. Ricky liked her very much. So did Hannie and the rest of the students. Ricky did not want to disappoint her.

"I know it is hard to pay attention today, girls and boys," said Ms. Colman. "But please try this afternoon. Right now it is almost lunchtime. So you may clear off your desks. After lunch, you will come back here to our room for recess. It is too wet to play outside."

"Boo and bullfrogs," Ricky heard Karen Brewer say. Ricky peered down his row of desks. Karen sat at the other end of it. He knew Karen wanted to play outside. So did Ricky. But they could not. They would have to play indoor games.

When lunch was over, the kids in Ms. Colman's class formed a line in the cafeteria. Ricky noticed that Karen was at the head of it. She usually was. The kids walked through the hall in their line. They entered their classroom. They saw that Ms.

Colman had set out some board games. And some math games. And some paper and markers and scissors.

Karen dove for the markers. "Hannie! Nancy!" she called to her best friends. "Come here! We can make paper jewelry." (Karen was so bossy.)

"No, *we* are going to make jewelry!" cried Leslie Morris and Jannie Gilbert.

"There is plenty of paper for everyone," said Ms. Colman quietly.

At the front of the room, Hank Reubens and Bobby Gianelli were drawing a picture of Natalie Springer on the chalkboard. Audrey Green was throwing an eraser at Ian Johnson. In the back of the room, Sara Ford and the twins, Tammy and Terri Barkan, were trying to play hopscotch. Chris Lamar was doodling on his sneakers with a marker.

The room was noisy. Nobody was playing with the games. A paper plane flew through the air.

Ms. Colman clapped her hands. "Boys and girls! May I have your attention, please? Class? . . . *Class!*"

The kids stopped what they were doing. They looked at their teacher.

"This is pandemonium," said Ms. Colman. "You are too loud and too wild. Please go to your seats. I think we need a story break." When the room was quiet, Ms. Colman said, "Ricky, would you please choose a book for us?"

Ricky grinned. "Sure," he said. He hurried to the reading corner behind Nancy and Karen. He knew just which book to choose. *Sloppy Sam* by Mr. Robert Bennett. Robert Bennett was Ricky's favorite author. And *Sloppy Sam* was Ricky's favorite book by his favorite author. The kids in Ms. Colman's class had heard it dozens of times, but they would not mind hearing it again. Robert Bennett's books were so, so funny. Ricky especially liked that Mr. Bennett wrote his books *and* drew the pictures for them.

Ricky handed *Sloppy Sam* to Ms. Colman. "Here," he said.

"Goody!" said Sara. "*Sloppy Sam* again."

"Cool," said Omar Harris.

And the kids settled down to listen to one of Mr. Bennett's giggle books.

2
AUTHOR DAY

"Good morning, girls and boys," said Ms. Colman.

Sara hurried to her seat. So did the other kids in Ms. Colman's room. Another Monday was about to begin.

"Chris, would you take attendance, please?" asked Ms. Colman. Chris walked proudly to the front of the room. Ms. Colman handed him her book. Then she collected homework papers. Finally, she said, "Class, I have something exciting to tell you."

Oh, goody, thought Karen. One of Ms. Colman's Surprising Announcements.

"In one month," Ms. Colman began,

P.E. 9:00 AM.

"we will have Author Day here at Stoney-brook Academy. Several authors will visit. They will talk about their books and about writing. Guess who is going to talk to the second- and third-graders."

Natalie Springer raised her hand. "Babar?" she suggested. (Her classmates covered their mouths and giggled.)

"No, not Babar," said Ms. Colman. "Babar is a character in a book. An author is a person who *writes* books. And the au-

thor who is going to visit us is . . . Robert Bennett."

"Robert Bennett!" cried Ricky. "He is an author *and* an artist."

"Cool!" said Tammy.

"Coming to our *school*?" asked Nancy Dawes.

"To our *class*room," Ms. Colman replied. "Right to our class."

Ricky could not believe this. Nobody could.

"Will he show us how he draws pictures?" asked Ricky.

"I think so," said Ms. Colman.

"Will he tell us how he thought up the idea for *Sloppy Sam*?" asked Sara.

"I think so."

"Can I bring my own book by Robert Bennett to school on Author Day?" asked Audrey. "I have a copy of *Awful Alligators* at home. Maybe Mr. Bennett could sign his name in it for me. I collect autographs."

"Unfortunately," said Ms. Colman, "that is one thing Mr. Bennett will not be able to do. He will be very, very busy on Author Day. He will not have time to sign books."

"Boo and bullfrogs," muttered Karen.

But Bobby said, "Oh, well. At least we get to meet him."

"Where does he live?" asked Jannie.

"How does he think up all those funny books?" asked Leslie.

"Those are very good questions,"

said Ms. Colman. "And you can ask Mr. Bennett himself on Author Day. I wonder, though, if Mr. Bennett might like to know your questions before Author Day. That way, he can think about the answers to them ahead of time. So in a few days, you will each write a letter to Mr. Bennett. You are also going to be writing stories of your own. You will work in pairs. We will choose one story to make into a big book to read to Mr. Bennett. We will read it to him at a party that the second-graders and third-graders will give Mr. Bennett in the library at the end of Author Day. While the story is being read, several of you will perform it. You will put on a skit. The students in the other classes will plan things for Mr. Bennett, too. We might also want to think about a gift we could make that we could give our guest at the party.

"As you can see," Ms. Colman went on, "we are going to be very busy before

Author Day. We have lots of things to plan and do."

Ricky smiled to himself. He could not wait for Author Day. It was going to be the most exciting thing that had ever happened in second grade.

3

THE FARTING PUPPY

Every morning, the kids in Ms. Colman's class had reading activities. Sometimes Ms. Colman read to the class. She would choose a good book and read a chapter from it each day. (Omar's favorite had been *James and the Giant Peach*, by Roald Dahl.) Sometimes the kids would break into groups and work on different activities. Sometimes they wrote in their workbooks. And sometimes they took turns reading stories aloud from their readers.

"Class," said Ms. Colman one morning, "please open your books to page

13

twenty-one. We are going to read the story that begins there."

The kids opened their books. They looked at the title on page twenty-one. It was "The Puppy Who Wished for a Girl."

Jannie liked the sound of that. So did the other kids.

"Okay, Hank," said Ms. Colman. "You may read first."

Hank began the story. It was about a puppy who had no home. More than anything, the puppy wished for a home and a family. She especially wished for a girl who would play with her and take care of her. Hank read the first page of the story. Tammy read the second page. Sara read the third page.

"Ricky," said Ms. Colman. "Will you read the fourth page?"

Ricky sat up tall. He cleared his throat. " 'The sun was shining,' " he began. " 'It was a beautiful day. The puppy smiled. She wanted to visit her new friend. So she farted across the lawn.' "

14

Ricky had read only half the page. He was supposed to finish it. But he stopped. He stopped because all around him the kids were laughing. He looked at Ms. Colman. She was smiling.

Ricky thought about what he had just read. "So she darted across the lawn." No, that was not quite it. He had said, "So she farted across the lawn." *Farted*. Ricky had said "farted" in front of everyone in his class. Even in front of his *teacher*.

Ricky looked at Hannie. She had covered her mouth with her hand. But Ricky knew she was laughing anyway. At the end of his row of desks, Karen was laughing so hard her face had turned red. At the front of the room, Hank and Bobby were laughing, too. Bobby had slid out of his chair onto the floor. Over by the windows, Leslie had laughed until her gum shot out of her mouth. It had stuck to her desk.

"Okay, class. That is enough," said Ms. Colman. (Ricky noticed that she was still smiling, though.) "Class," Ms. Colman had to say again. And then, "Boys and girls, *please*. Please settle down."

When the kids finally stopped laughing, Ms. Colman said, "Ricky, you may continue."

Ricky shook his head. "No."

"No?" said Mrs. Colman.

"No. I do not want to read aloud."

"Okay. That is all right, Ricky. Natalie, it is your turn, then."

Ricky slumped in his seat. He slumped

until his head was touching the back of his chair. He had an idea that he was going to be hearing farting jokes for a long, long time. So Ricky made a decision. He was never going to read aloud again. Not ever. Ms. Colman did not know this yet. And his classmates did not know it yet. But Ricky would show them.

That afternoon, Ms. Colman wrote a math problem on the board. "Ricky, will you please read the problem for us?" she asked.

Ricky shook his head. "No." Then he added, "I am not going to read aloud anymore. Not ever."

Ms. Colman looked surprised. But she did not say anything. The kids looked surprised, too.

Good, thought Ricky. I will teach them.

Ricky would not read his name from a list on the board. He would not read the lunch menu when Karen asked if they were going to have pizza on Friday. Ricky was mad at everybody. He was especially mad at Hannie, Karen, Hank, Bobby, and Leslie. All the kids had laughed at him that morning. But they had laughed the loudest of all.

4

DEAR MR. BENNETT

It was a sleepy Monday morning. The kids in Ms. Colman's class were having a little trouble paying attention. Audrey was counting POGs inside her desk. Ian was staring out the window. Leslie had turned around and was watching Omar draw a cartoon picture of a superhero. Jannie was peering through the doorway, trying to see what was going on in Mr. Berger's class next door.

But Ms. Colman woke everyone up. "Girls and boys," she said, "it is time to write our letters to Mr. Bennett." She handed out paper.

19

Terri raised her hand. "What are we supposed to say?" she asked.

"Class?" Ms. Colman replied. "What could we say in our letters?"

"We could tell Mr. Bennett about ourselves," suggested Sara.

"Like who's in our family," said Chris.

"And if we have pets," said Jannie.

"If we have farting puppies," added Leslie.

Ricky stuck his tongue out at Leslie. And Ms. Colman said, "Now, now."

"We have to remember to ask questions," said Karen.

"Right," agreed Ms. Colman. "Think of questions to ask Mr. Bennett."

Chris Lamar stared at the blank paper in front of him. He wrote DEAR MR. Then he stopped. He raised his hand. "How do you spell 'Bennett'?" he asked. He could hear a "B" sound and an "N" sound and a "T" sound. But he was pretty sure Bennett was not spelled BNT.

Ms. Colman wrote *BENNETT* on the board.

"Thank you," said Chris. He copied *BENNETT* onto his paper. Then he chewed on his pencil and thought for awhile.

Next to Chris, Audrey was staring at her paper. So far she had written *DEAR MR. BENNETT, HOW ARE YOU? I AM FINE.* Now she was stuck.

Karen was not stuck. She had lots of questions for Mr. Bennett. She was busy

writing. When she finished her letter, it read:

DEAR MR. BENNETT,
1. WHERE DO YOU LIVE?
2. HOW OLD ARE YOU?
3. ARE YOU MARRIED?
4. DO YOU HAVE ANY KIDS?
5. DO YOU LIKE PETS?
6. HOW MANY BOOKS HAVE YOU WRITTEN?
7. WHEN DID YOU WRITE YOUR FIRST BOOK?
8. DID YOU LIKE TO WRITE WHEN YOU WERE IN SECOND GRADE?
9. WHO WAS YOUR FAVORITE TEACHER?
10. WHAT IS YOUR FAVORITE TV SHOW?
11. ARE YOU FAMOUS?

LOVE, KAREN BREWER

Ricky thought for a long time. Finally he wrote:

DEar Mr. BENnett,
    I am Ricky TORRES. I am 7.
I go to Stnebruk Akadme.
Everone here is mean. They
laff at You and make fun if
you make a mistake do not mak
a mistak when you visit here.
  Your freind,
  Ricky Torres
P.S. I LIKE YOUR Books.

Ms. Colman made Ricky start his letter over. Ricky did not mind too much. Mostly, he had just wanted Ms. Colman to know how angry he was.

When the kids in Ms. Colman's class had finished their letters and copied them neatly, Ms. Colman said, "Now we are ready to mail our letters to Mr. Bennett." She put the letters into a big envelope. Then she said, "Ian, Sara, I have an important job for you. If you will take this envelope to the office, the secretary will mail it to Mr. Bennett for us."

Ian and Sara grinned. They stood up. Ms. Colman handed them the envelope. And they walked proudly down the hall with it.

5

JUICY LUCY

That afternoon, Ms. Colman said to her students, "Class, today we are going to make our own books. When they are finished, we will choose one to read to Mr. Bennett on Author Day. You will work in pairs — in teams of two people. Each pair will write and illustrate a story of their own. I will choose the pairs. When I say your name, please find your partner. Okay. Jannie and Bobby. Omar and Tammy. Nancy and Hank. Karen and Terri. Ricky and Natalie. Hannie and Chris. Leslie and Ian. Sara and Audrey." Ms. Colman looked around the room. Her students were scrambling to find places where they could work. Some of them sat at desks. Some of them sat on the floor.

"Remember," Ms. Colman continued, "you are making a book. So you need a story *and* pictures. I will hand out crayons."

Ricky looked at Natalie. Natalie was not his favorite person. She was sloppy and she forgot things. But she was okay.

"Well," said Natalie. "What do you want to do, Ricky? Write or draw?" (Ricky was not Natalie's favorite person, either. But he was okay.)

"Write the story," replied Ricky. "I like making up stories."

"Goody," said Natalie. "I would rather draw pictures."

"Now let me see." Ricky thought and thought. At last he said, "I know! I will write a story about a goose named Lucy."

Ricky bent over the paper. He began to write. He scribbled away.

"What are you writing?" asked Natalie.

Ricky shoved the paper at her. "Here. You read it."

"No, you. I will start drawing a picture while I listen."

"Sorry," said Ricky. "I do not read aloud anymore."

Natalie scowled. Ricky was a big pain. She leaned over to see his story. It was about a fat goose named Lucy. Lucy lived on a farm. She was so fat that the farmer and his wife had nicknamed her Juicy Lucy. They said she would make a tasty goose dinner one day.

That was all Ricky had written so far. Natalie looked at the first sentence of his story. It read: "Once there lived a big fat goose named Lucy." So Natalie began a picture of Lucy.

Ricky scribbled away.

"Now what is happening in the story?" asked Natalie.

"See for yourself," said Ricky. He handed her another page.

Natalie read on. Lucy heard the farmer talking about a "dinner date." She thought she was to be taken out to dinner by a fine goose gentleman. So she began to get ready for her date.

"Cool," said Natalie. "I cannot wait to read the end of the story."

The other students worked on their stories, too. Jannie and Bobby started one called, "Backwards Day." Hannie and Chris worked on one called, "Sailing Out to Sea." Sara and Audrey had trouble thinking of something to write about. Finally they began a story called, "The Little Flower."

Natalie drew and drew. She drew a picture of the farmer and the farmer's wife. She drew a picture of the farmer dreaming of the tasty goose dinner. She drew a picture of Lucy dreaming of the fine goose gentleman who would be her dinner date.

"May I read the rest of the story, please?" Natalie asked Ricky.

Ricky handed her the last two pages.

Natalie read the part in which Lucy found out she was going to *be* dinner, not go out for dinner. She read about how Lucy outsmarted the farmer and ran away. Finally she read, " 'Lucy ran all the way to a pond. There she found a fine goose gentleman who asked her to stay at the pond with him forever. So she did.' "

"Write 'The End,' " Natalie said to Ricky.

Ricky added *The End* to his story.

"That," said Natalie, "is one of the best stories I have ever read."

"Thank you," replied Ricky. "And I like your pictures."

THE WINNER

One by one, the teams in Ms. Colman's class finished their books. Ms. Colman collected them. "During the next two days," she said, "I will read each of the stories aloud to you. When you have heard them all, you will vote on the one to read to Mr. Bennett on Author Day. Then we will begin the other projects."

The next day, Ms. Colman read "Sailing Out to Sea," "The Little Flower," and two other stories to her students. On Wednesday, she read "Backwards Day," "Juicy Lucy," and the last two stories.

"And now," she said, "it is time to vote. I will read the titles of the stories to you. Please vote for just one, for your favorite."

Uh-oh, thought Ricky. That will never work. Every team is going to vote for their own story. We will have an eight-way tie. Then what will happen?

Ricky scowled. But he rested his head on his arms, the way Ms. Colman had told her students to do while they voted.

"Okay, class," said Ms. Colman. "Here are the stories."

Ricky waited to hear Ms. Colman call out, "Juicy Lucy."

He raised his hand.

"Well," said Ms. Colman a few minutes later. "We have a winner."

We *do*? thought Ricky. He lifted his head. He looked at the blackboard.

Next to "Sailing Out to Sea" was the number 2. Next to "Backwards Day" was another 2. Next to "Juicy Lucy" was a 12.

Twelve? Twelve kids had voted for "Juicy Lucy"? Ricky grinned at Natalie in the front of the room. Natalie waved at him.

"Congratulations, Natalie and Ricky!" said Ms. Colman. "Your story has been chosen for Author Day. You will make it into a big book. You will be in charge of turning it into a skit. And of course, you will read it to Mr. Bennett. It is a fine story. You did a wonderful job."

"Thank you," said Natalie politely.

But Ricky did not say anything. He had just thought of something. He had realized he better make sure Natalie would be the one who would read the story. Because Ricky would not do it. He had not changed his mind about reading aloud. He had meant what he said.

At lunchtime, Ricky found Natalie's table in the cafeteria.

"What are you doing here?" she asked him. Natalie was sitting with Terri and Tammy and Audrey.

"I have to talk to you," replied Ricky.

Natalie slurped her milk. "About what?"

"About our story. Will you read it to Mr. Bennett on Author Day?"

"*Read* it?" repeated Natalie. "No. You wrote it. And I drew the pictures. So I will be the one to hold the book, turn the pages, and show off the beautiful drawings — while you read."

"No way," said Ricky. "I am not going to read."

"Well, neither am I."

"I do not have to."

"You better," said Natalie.

"Yeah," said Audrey.

"No way," said Ricky.

"Yes way," said Tammy.

"Talk to Ms. Colman about it," suggested Natalie.

"All right, I will." Ricky stood up. Girls. What pains. "You got carrots in your teeth," Ricky called to Natalie as he left.

Ricky looked around the cafeteria. Where was Ms. Colman? Finally he saw her talking to some other teachers at the back of the room.

"Ms. Colman?" said Ricky, when he had made his way to her.

"Ricky? Is anything wrong? Why haven't you eaten your lunch?"

"Because I need to talk to you. I am not going to read 'Juicy Lucy' on Author Day. I will not read aloud."

Ms. Colman sighed. "Why don't you eat your lunch, Ricky? Then we will talk quietly together. I will come find you in fifteen minutes."

THE DEAL

Fifteen minutes later, Ms. Colman and Ricky were walking back to their classroom. Ricky's friends were having fun on the playground. Ricky sighed. He wished he were outside with them.

"Okay, Ricky," said Ms. Colman. "Why don't you sit here, near me, in Hank's seat?" Ms. Colman sat at her own desk. "Now, then," she began, "I know you have been upset. I know you are embarrassed about the mistake you made the other day. And I have tried to be patient with you. I want to understand you. So tell me what is going on now."

"I am mad. And I am never going to

36

read aloud again," said Ricky.

"Never again is a very long time," replied Ms. Colman. "I do not think you *really* mean never again."

"Yes, I do."

"Ricky, this is getting out of hand. Sometimes I will need to hear you read aloud. I need to hear all my students read aloud. I cannot ask your classmates to do something, and then tell you that you do not have to do it. That is not fair to anybody."

Ricky did not say anything. He stared down at his shirt buttons.

"Very well," said Ms. Colman. "I cannot force you to do something you do not want to do. But I must tell you that if you will not read 'Juicy Lucy' aloud at the party on Author Day, then you may not come to Author Day. You will come to school, of course, but you will go to the resource room. If you change your mind, though, and decide to read, then you may come to Author Day. Is that a deal?"

"Deal," replied Ricky. Then he muttered, "I am not going to read my story."

"All right. That is your choice," said Ms. Colman. "I want to make something clear to you, though. Whether or not you come to Author Day, you must do all of the Author Day classwork. You and Natalie will still make the big book. And you will still work on the 'Juicy Lucy' play. Do you understand?"

Ricky nodded. "Yes."

"And you may change your mind

about Author Day any time. You may even change it on the morning of Author Day."

"Okay," said Ricky. "But I am not going to read." Then Ricky said to himself, "Even though I really *really* REALLY want to meet Mr. Bennett."

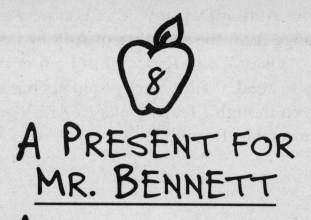

A Present for Mr. Bennett

After recess that day, Ms. Colman divided her students into several groups.

"We have so many things to do before Author Day," said Ms. Colman. "Sara, your group is going to make decorations for our classroom. Chris, your group is going to make decorations for the party in the library. Nancy, your group is going to think of a gift to make for Mr. Bennett. We will give him the gift at the party. And Natalie and Ricky, you two are going to start turning 'Juicy Lucy' into a giant book."

"Decorations," said Sara to Jannie and Tammy and Hank and Ian. "What kind of decorations should we make?"

"Not party decorations," replied Hank. "The other group gets to make those."

"We could make a sign that says 'Welcome, Mr. Bennett,'" suggested Ian.

"We could make paper flowers," said Tammy.

"Paper flowers? No way," said Jannie. "That is stupid."

"We could draw pictures of the characters in Mr. Bennett's books," said Sara. "Like Sloppy Sam."

"Or an awful alligator!" exclaimed Hank.

Chris's group began making their party decorations right away. They started with paper chains. Then they decided to cut out a bunch of paper balloons. They planned to tie real strings to the balloons.

Nancy's group had some trouble.

"What do you give an author?" wondered Audrey. "A *famous* author?"

"Ms. Colman said we have to *make* the gift," added Karen. "I wonder if she meant that. Ms. Colman? Ms. Colman? . . . Ms. Colman!"

"Karen, indoor voice, please," said Ms. Colman. She sat down with Nancy's group. "Do you need help?" she asked.

"Do we really have to *make* Mr. Bennett's gift?" said Karen.

"I think it would be nice."

"But what can we make?" asked Audrey.

"Maybe something with Popsicle

sticks," said Omar. "Like a box for his pencils."

"I bet he writes on a computer," said Nancy.

"Then how about a pillow for him to sit on while he works?" suggested Omar.

"A pillow? No way. I am not sewing a pillow," said Bobby.

"I know you will think of something," said Ms. Colman.

Ms. Colman stood up. She watched Natalie and Ricky for awhile. She had given them an enormous blank book. The pages were made of heavy cardboard. Ricky was copying his story onto the pages, and Natalie was copying her pictures.

Ms. Colman smiled. She was proud of her students. And she was looking forward to Author Day as much as they were.

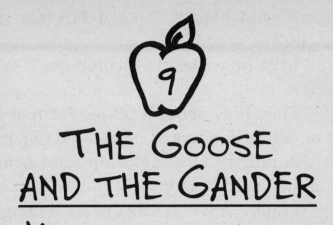

THE GOOSE
AND THE GANDER

Mr. Bennett's visit was getting closer and closer. The kids in Ms. Colman's room had been working hard. Sara's group had finished the decorations for the classroom. Ms. Colman had set them carefully in a large box marked CLASS DECS. Chris's group had finished their decorations, too. Ms. Colman had put them in another box, marked PARTY DECS. Nancy's group had finished their present. It had taken a long time for them to decide on a gift. At last they had made a book for Mr. Bennett. But they did not write a story on the pages they stapled together. Instead, they left the pages blank. The book was a diary for Mr.

Bennett. He could write about a trip he took or a special event or maybe his visit to Stoneybrook Academy. The kids decorated the cover of the diary, and put a ribbon in it for a bookmark. They were very proud of their gift.

Ricky and Natalie had finished their big book. That had been a hard job. Ricky did not want any mistakes in it. Natalie got tired of copying her pictures. But they worked until they were proud of what they had done. Now the giant book was propped in the front of the classroom.

One afternoon, Ms. Colman said to her students, "It is time to begin our next project for Author Day. It is time to make 'Juicy Lucy' into a play. Natalie and Ricky, you are in charge of the play."

"Cool," said Ricky. (He was getting an idea.)

"I will help you," Ms. Colman went on, "if you need a hand. But you are in charge. This is what you need to think about. On Author Day, someone will read the story of 'Juicy Lucy' aloud. Natalie will hold up the big book and turn the pages so everyone can see the pictures. Next to her, several of you will act out the story. You will not be speaking, since someone will be *reading* the story. But you might have costumes or props. Do you know what props are?"

"Are they things you carry?" asked Karen.

"In a way. Yes. They are things you need for the play that are not parts of your

costumes. The farmer might need a pail. The goose gentleman might need an umbrella. You might need food for the dinner.

"So Ricky and Natalie, your job is to choose actors for the skit, and other kids to help you with the costumes and props. Okay?"

Ricky and Natalie nodded importantly. Then Ricky stood up. He walked to the front of the room. Natalie joined him.

"All right. Who wants to be Juicy Lucy?" asked Ricky.

Four hands shot up. Three of them belonged to Hannie, Karen, and Leslie. They had laughed especially loudly about the farting puppy. Ricky looked at the fourth person. "Okay, Audrey. You can be Lucy," he said. "Now who wants to be the gander, Lucy's dinner date?"

Three hands shot up. Two of them belonged to Bobby and Hank.

"Omar, you may be the gander," said Ricky.

The kids stopped raising their hands. Even so, Ricky and Natalie chose Ian to be the farmer, and Terri to be his wife. They chose Chris to be Lucy's goose-friend at the end of the story. They chose Nancy and Sara to be the farmer's daughters. They choose Tammy and Jannie to be animals on the farm.

At last only Karen, Hannie, Leslie, Bobby, and Hank were left.

"What about us?" asked Leslie.

"You girls can be in charge of costumes," said Ricky bossily. "And you boys can be in charge of props."

"But I wanted to be *in* the play!" cried Karen.

"And I do *not* want to be in the play!" exclaimed Nancy.

"Too bad," said Ricky.

"Wait a minute," said Natalie suddenly. She narrowed her eyes at Ricky. "How come you did not let these guys in the play? Tell the truth," she added.

"Well," said Ricky, "because they laughed the loudest when I said, um . . ." Ricky paused. "When I made the mistake about the dog." (Ricky was not about to say "farting" again.)

"No fair!" said Hank.

"It was no fair when you laughed at me," said Ricky.

"Uh-oh," said Ms. Colman.

10
RUN FOR YOUR LIFE!

Ms. Colman stood between Ricky and Natalie. "I think we better start over," she said to her students. "But first I would like Karen, Hannie, Leslie, Bobby, and Hank to apologize to Ricky for laughing."

"I'm sorry," said the kids.

"And now I would like Ricky to apologize to Karen, Hannie, Leslie, Bobby, and Hank."

"*Why*?" cried Ricky. "I do not want them in the play. And it is *my* play."

"First of all," said Ms. Colman, "it is your play *and* Natalie's. Not just yours. Second, if you did not choose Karen, Hannie, Leslie, Bobby, and Hank to be in the play because you think they are not right for any parts, that is fine. But if you did not choose them because you wanted to hurt their feelings the way they hurt yours, then that is not fine. And I think that is what you did. So please apologize, Ricky."

"Sorry," muttered Ricky.

"Okay. Let's start over again," said Ms. Colman. "And Natalie, this time I would like you to speak up when you and Ricky are choosing the characters. You have good ideas. Ricky, please forget about who laughed. Choose the kids you think would be best for each role or job."

Ricky and Natalie began again. When they had finished, Omar was still the gander, but Leslie was Lucy. Bobby and Terri were the farmer and his wife, Chris was still the goose-friend, Audrey and Sara were the farmer's daughters, and Karen and Hank were the farm animals. Jannie, Ian, and Nancy were in charge of the costumes, and Tammy and Hannie were in charge of the props.

51

"Good," Nancy whispered to Hannie. "I really did not want to be in the play."

"And I really did," Karen whispered back.

"Ahem! No talking!" called Natalie from the front of the room.

"Yeah. It is time to start rehearsing," said Ricky.

"Already?" asked Ian. "Shouldn't we plan the costumes first? Author Day is coming soon. Jannie and Nancy and I need to know what stuff to look for."

"And Hannie and I need to know what props to look for," said Tammy.

"Okay, okay. We will have a meeting first," said Natalie.

Five days later, the kids in Ms. Colman's class held their first dress rehearsal. (Mr. Bennett's visit was just two days away.)

"All right," said Natalie. She and Ricky were standing at the front of the room again. Their classmates were sitting on the floor. The desks had been pushed against the back wall. Ms. Colman was sitting with the kids. "Prop people," Natalie went on, "did you bring all the props?"

"Yes!" called Hannie.

"And costume people," said Ricky, "did you bring everything?"

"Yes!" called Jannie.

"Then everybody into your costumes," said Natalie.

Jannie, Ian, and Nancy handed out the costumes. Leslie put on the red kerchief that Lucy always wore. The farmer and his wife slipped overalls over their school clothes. Then they put on straw hats. The farm animals put on mittens and masks, and tails made from rope. Tammy and Hannie handed out the props. Soon the story characters looked just the way Natalie had drawn them.

Ms. Colman smiled. "Everyone looks wonderful!" she said. "Okay. Ricky, are

you ready to read the story?"

"Nope," said Ricky.

Natalie rolled her eyes. "Then *I* will read it," she said. "But I am *not* going to read it on Author Day." (She glared at Ricky.)

The play began. Leslie in her red kerchief posed with the farm family. (Bobby's hat kept slipping over his eyes.) Then Leslie posed with the farm animals. (The cow's tail fell off.) Leslie dreamed of her dinner date.

"Omar, you are supposed to sit at that table now!" Ricky whispered loudly. "You are the dinner date."

"I am trying to sit. But my tail feathers will not stay on!"

Natalie kept reading the story. " 'Run for your life!' " she read.

Nothing happened. No one moved.

"Leslie, you are supposed to start running around the room now," said Ricky. "The farmer is after you."

"Oh. I forgot," said Leslie.

"Cut!" cried Natalie.

"Do over!" cried Ricky. "This is horrible."

But Ms. Colman smiled. "I am sure it will be fine," she said.

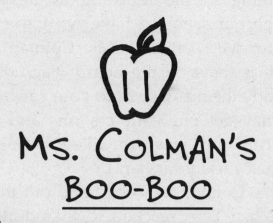

MS. COLMAN'S BOO-BOO

It was the day before Author Day. The kids were getting very excited. They had had another rehearsal that morning, and "Juicy Lucy" had gone much better. Now they were sitting at their desks after recess. On Ms. Colman's desk was a stack of colored paper. Ricky had a feeling Ms. Colman was about to give them a fun project.

Sure enough, Ms. Colman said, "Class, Mr. Bennett will be here tomorrow. We would like to make him feel at home at Stoneybrook Academy. So we are going to make welcome cards for him. We will hang them in the hallway. He will see the cards first thing in the morning as he walks through our school. I have written a message for Mr. Bennett," Ms. Colman went on. "It is there on the board. Each of you will copy the message onto your card. Then you may get out your crayons and color your card any way you like. If you need help just raise your hand."

Ms. Colman let Terri hand out the paper. When Terri reached Ricky's desk, she said, "What color would you like?"

"Hmm. Green, I think," said Ricky. "No, wait. Yellow. No, blue." Ricky wanted to choose just the right color for Mr. Bennett. But he did not know what color famous authors liked. Finally he said, "Blue, I guess."

Terri gave Ricky a piece of blue paper. Ricky set to work. He folded the paper in half slowly and carefully. Then he found a pencil. He began to copy Ms. Colman's message onto the inside of the card. He wrote very lightly so he could erase his mistakes. Then he looked in his desk. He found a ballpoint pen. Ms. Colman did not usually let her students write in pen. But Ricky decided this was a special occasion. He wanted his card to look grown-up (since it would be hanging in the hall where everyone would see it). Besides, he had already written in pencil. He was just going to trace over it with the pen.

Ricky bent over his paper. He stuck his tongue between his teeth. He began to trace the words.

Dear . . . Mr. . . . Bennett . . . thank . . . you . . .

Ricky stopped writing. He stared down at his paper. Then he looked up at the board. He squinted to make sure he saw what he thought he saw. Finally he called out, "Hey, Ms. Colman! You made a mistake! And I almost copied it onto my card. In ink," he added. "See? You wrote, 'Dear Mr. Bennett, thank you coming to

Stoneybrook Academy.' You left out the 'for.' "

"Oops," said Ms. Colman.

"Oh, no. And I just copied it!" cried Sara. "In red crayon."

"I copied it in *marker*!" exclaimed Karen. "Boo and bullfrogs."

"How many of you already copied the message in something you cannot erase?" asked Ms. Colman. She looked at her students.

Sara, Karen, and four other kids raised their hands.

"I am very sorry," said Ms. Colman. "That was my mistake. Let me fix it on the board so the rest of you do not make it, too. Then we will figure out what to do." Ms. Colman picked up a piece of chalk.

"Hey!" Karen cried. "Hey, Ricky!"

"Indoor voice, Karen," said Ms. Colman.

"But Ms. Colman, Ricky read aloud! He read what you wrote on the board. And

if he had not done that, then we would have put up all these cards with mistakes in them. Ricky saved us."

Terri turned around in her seat. She whispered, "Thanks, Ricky. I would not have wanted that to happen."

"Thanks, Ricky," said a few other kids.

Ricky grinned. He felt like a hero.

At the end of the day, he waited by Ms. Colman's desk.

"Yes, Ricky?" she said.

"I have decided something," said

Ricky. "I have decided I would like to read my story to Mr. Bennett tomorrow."

"That's wonderful!" exclaimed Ms. Colman. "Good for you, Ricky. I will see you tomorrow — on Author Day."

12

MR. ROBERT
BENNETT

When Natalie woke up on Author Day, she was excited. She could feel butterflies in her tummy. She dressed in a rush. When she was finished, her skirt was on crooked and her socks were falling down. But Natalie did not care. She pushed her glasses up her nose.

"Hurry!" she said to her father. "I want to get to school early. Today I am going to show Mr. Bennett my beautiful pictures."

Ricky was in the bathroom. He was brushing his teeth. He watched himself in the mirror. He wondered what he would say to Mr. Bennett when he met him that day.

Splat. Ricky spit out the toothpaste. Then he looked in the mirror again. "Pleased to meet you, Mr. Bennett," he said. "I mean, how do you do? I mean, it is *nice* to meet you. . . . I was wondering. How did you get here today? In a limousine or a helicopter?"

Karen Brewer stepped out of her front door. She was wearing a new dress and her tappy black party shoes. She had tied a ribbon in her hair. She felt like a princess.

" 'Bye, Mommy!" Karen called. She ran across the lawn to Nancy's house next door. "Nancy, Nancy!" Karen yelled. "Hurry up! Let's go! Author Day is here!"

When Chris reached Stoneybrook
Academy, he walked proudly to his classroom. On the walls of the hallway hung the
cards for Mr. Bennett. They looked nice
and welcoming. Ahead, he could see Hank
in the doorway.

"Come on, Chris!" Hank called. "We
are going to decorate the room now!"

Chris hurried down the hall. Ms. Colman was standing at her desk. She was
leaning over the box marked CLASS DECS.

She handed out the things that Sara's group had made.

"After we have decorated our room, we will decorate the library," Ms. Colman said. "Mr. Bennett will be here at about ten-thirty."

It was a busy morning. The kids tidied up their room. Audrey and Omar wrapped the present for Mr. Bennett. Chris's group put up the decorations in the library.

At ten o'clock, Ms. Colman said, "Boys and girls, you have time to rehearse 'Juicy Lucy' again. Why don't you get out your costumes and props? Natalie and Ricky will be in charge for awhile."

Natalie and Ricky grinned at each other. They moved to the front of the room.

"You will have to rehearse up here by the blackboard," Ricky said to his classmates. "We do not have time to move the desks around."

"Are you ready?" Natalie asked the kids. "Okay, action."

Ricky began reading his story.

Leslie posed with the farm family. (Bobby's hat did not slip over his eyes.)

Leslie posed with the farm animals. (All of their tails stayed on.)

Omar remembered to sit at the dinner table.

"Run for your life!" called Ricky. Leslie ran around the room, with Bobby after her.

When the play was over, Ms. Colman clapped her hands. "Wonderful!" she said. "That was just wonderful. Mr. Bennett is going to love the play. Ricky, you read very nicely.

"Okay, class. Leave your costumes and props in this box. I will take them to the library later. Please go back to your seats now."

The kids returned to their seats. Ricky looked at his watch. It was almost ten-thirty. His heart began to beat faster.

The next thing he knew, someone was knocking on the door to the classroom. The door opened. A tall man with a beard stepped inside. He was carrying a briefcase.

"Boys and girls," said Ms. Colman, "I would like you to meet Mr. Robert Bennett."

13

POPCORN

"Welcome, Mr. Bennett," said Ms. Colman. "Welcome to our class."

Ms. Colman's room was very, very quiet.

"Girls and boys," said Ms. Colman, "please say hello to Mr. Bennett."

"Hello," whispered the kids.

Hannie did not say anything at all. Her mouth hung open.

Hank just stared. Before him stood a real live author.

Mr. Bennett was wearing blue jeans and a white shirt and a necktie. And sneakers. Chris liked the way he looked. It was very friendly. But he had hoped the author might wear a tuxedo.

Mr. Bennett grinned. "Hi, kids," he said. "You are awfully quiet. I bet you are not always this quiet."

"They certainly are not," said Ms. Colman.

"Well, there is no need to be shy. I have never bitten anybody. At least not anybody I can remember."

In the back of the room, Karen giggled. She liked Mr. Bennett.

"Now," began Mr. Bennett. "Let me tell you a little about myself."

Mr. Bennett told the kids that he had written seventeen books. "My first was *Sloppy Sam*. I think I look like Sloppy Sam." He told the kids what his favorite book was. He asked what theirs was. Then he said, "Do you have any questions for me?"

Ricky wanted to raise his hand. He had a lot of questions for Mr. Bennett. But he was still feeling shy. So were his classmates.

"I know you have questions. I read your letters," said Mr. Bennett.

Finally Ricky raised his hand. "How old were you when you wrote *Sloppy Sam*?" he asked.

"I was twenty-seven," said Mr. Bennett.

"Could you draw good pictures when you were seven?" asked Natalie.

"*Pretty* good ones," replied Mr. Bennett.

"Are you working on a new story now?" asked Omar.

Mr. Bennett grinned. "I just finished one. It is called *Cosmic Kitten*. It is in my briefcase." He pointed to his briefcase.

Audrey raised her hand. "Um, Mr. Bennett, would you like to meet our guinea pig?" she asked. "He is right over there. His name is Hootie."

Mr. Bennett said he would very much like to meet Hootie. So Audrey let him hold him for awhile.

When Hootie was back in his cage, Mr.

Bennett pulled some things out of his briefcase. He showed the kids in Ms. Colman's class how a picture book is made. He showed them how he wrote his stories. He showed them drawings he had made for *Cosmic Kitten*. He showed them what a book cover looks like before it goes on a book.

Then he said, "Kids, do you know what people ask me more than anything else? They ask me how I think up my characters. Well, now I am going to show you just how I do that. We are going to create a character together." Mr. Bennett propped up a huge pad of paper on Ms. Colman's chair. He put some markers on her desk. Then he said, "Okay. What does our character look like?"

The kids thought for a moment. Finally, Hank said, "Like a chimp!"

"But he has a big poofy tail," Jannie called out.

"And hooves instead of feet," said Terri.

Mr. Bennett drew a monkey with a

beautiful fat tail and horse hooves.

"And he always wears a hat!" cried Ian. "Because he has to stay out of the sun. He is sensitive."

"He lives in a castle," added Sara.

Mr. Bennett drew the hat and the castle.

The kids named their character Popcorn.

Finally Mr. Bennett looked at his watch. "I am afraid I must leave," he said. "But I will see you this afternoon. I enjoyed talking to you."

Mr. Bennett packed up his briefcase. He hurried off. But he left Popcorn behind for the kids.

"How special," said Ms. Colman. "We will have to frame Popcorn. For now, we will put him on the bulletin board."

Ricky sighed. He gazed at Popcorn. This had been the most wonderful morning of his life.

GOOD-BYE, MR. BENNETT

The visit with Mr. Bennett had sped by. The rest of the day dragged by. It felt like hours and hours and hours before it was time to line up and walk to the library. But finally the kids in Ms. Colman's class were on their way to the party. Nancy knew she was supposed to walk in the hallway, but she could not help skipping just a little.

The kids walked through the door to the library. Mr. Berger's second-graders were already there. So were the third-graders. They were sitting on the floor. Ms. Colman's kids joined them.

Tammy looked around the room. She

looked at the beautiful decorations. She saw four wrapped presents on the librarian's desk. And the box with the costumes and props.

Mr. Bennett was not there yet.

A few moments later he walked into the room with the librarian.

"Hello again!" he said.

Mr. Bennett was given a place of honor. He sat in the librarian's chair.

"Now it is our turn to entertain you," Ms. Colman said to Mr. Bennett. "First, we have some gifts for you."

One by one, a student from each of the classes presented Mr. Bennett with a gift. Nancy gave him the present from Ms. Colman's class.

"Oh, a diary!" exclaimed Mr. Bennett. "How useful. Thank you very much."

Nancy grinned. She did not feel nervous around Mr. Bennett anymore.

"And now," said Ms. Colman, "we have some things to show you."

The third-graders went first. One class

sang a song they had written for Mr. Bennett. The other class recited a poem for him. The kids in Mr. Berger's class played charades. They made Mr. Bennett guess which book titles they were acting out. They were titles of books Mr. Bennett had written.

At last it was time for "Juicy Lucy." Ricky could feel his heart pounding. He and Natalie carried their book to the front of the room. Nearby, their classmates were slipping into their costumes.

When everyone was ready, Ricky said, "We are pleased to present 'Juicy Lucy.' This is a story I wrote. Natalie drew the pictures. While I read the story, the other kids are going to act it out."

Ricky took a deep breath. He glanced at Leslie in her kerchief. He hoped she was ready. He hoped everyone was ready. He hoped no one made a mistake. He especially hoped he would not say "fart" in front of Mr. Bennett.

"Juicy Lucy," Ricky began.

Natalie opened the book. She turned to the first page.

" 'Once,' " Ricky read, " 'there lived a big fat goose named Lucy.' "

Leslie stepped next to Natalie. She took a bow.

Ricky read on. He read why Lucy was called Juicy Lucy. He read about the gander and the dinner date. He read about the wild goose chase and Lucy's escape and her new friend. Finally he said, "The end."

Ricky looked at Mr. Bennett. Mr. Bennett was smiling. "Bravo!" he said. He began to clap his hands. Everyone else began to clap, too. Ricky smiled. Then he grinned.

"That was wonderful," said Mr. Bennett.

"And now," Ms. Colman went on, "it is almost time for Mr. Bennett to leave. So let's have our refreshments. Then we must say good-bye."

The kids groaned.

"Boo and bullfrogs," said Karen Brewer.

Ms. Colman and Mr. Berger and the third-grade teachers stood up. They served punch and cookies. Soon, Ms. Colman was handing Mr. Bennett the welcome cards that had been hanging in the hall. Then she said, "Boys and girls, what do you say to our visitor?"

"Thank you, Mr. Bennett!" cried the kids. "Good-bye!"

THE FUTURE AUTHOR

Author Day was over. The kids could not believe it. One by one their classes left the library. Ms. Colman's class was last. "Good-bye!" the kids called again to Mr. Bennett. They watched him stride out of the library and down the hall.

"Please line up at the door now," said Ms. Colman to her students. "School is almost over. The bell is about to ring."

The kids scurried to line up. But not Ricky. He took one last look around the library. He looked at the chair Mr. Bennett had sat in. Then he looked at the librarian's desk. Leaning against it was Mr. Bennett's briefcase.

"Ms. Colman! Ms. Colman!" called Ricky.

Ms. Colman was already in the hall. She poked her head back in the room.

"Is something the matter, Ricky?"

"Mr. Bennett left his briefcase here! The one with his brand-new story in it."

"Oh, my goodness," said Ms. Colman. "Good for you for noticing that, Ricky. See if you can catch Mr. Bennett before he leaves school. Take the briefcase to the office. Mr. Bennett is probably there."

Ricky grabbed the briefcase. He ran through the hall with it. He knew he was not supposed to run. A patrol or a teacher might catch him at it. But Ricky had a good excuse. I will just say that I have the famous author's briefcase, he thought.

Pant, pant, pant.

Ricky skidded into the office.

Mr. Metz, one of the secretaries, was sitting at his desk.

"Mr. Metz! Is Mr. Bennett still here?" cried Ricky. "He left his briefcase behind! I have to give it to him."

"He just left," said Mr. Metz. "He is on his way to the parking lot."

"Thanks!" called Ricky.

Ricky dashed back to the hall. He ran to the doorway. He was thinking, The parking lot. I guess Mr. Bennett came in a limousine.

But when Ricky reached the parking lot, he did not see a limousine. He looked everywhere. All he saw were station wagons and vans, one truck, and an orange Volkswagen.

Standing beside the orange Volkswagen was Mr. Bennett. He was pulling a key chain from his pocket.

Where was the limo? Ricky wondered. Where was the limo driver? He could not believe that the famous author drove his own orange Volkswagen.

"Mr. Bennett?" Ricky called. Mr. Bennett turned around. "Mr. Bennett, you forgot your briefcase."

Mr. Bennett smacked his hand to his

forehead. "I would forget my head if it were not attached to my neck. Thank you so much."

"You're welcome. I know your new story is in it. That is very important. . . . Mr. Bennett? Thank you for coming to our school."

"It was my pleasure. I enjoy meeting the kids who read my books. Your name is Ricky, isn't it?" Ricky nodded. "And you read the story about the goose. 'Juicy Lucy.' That is a great title. I wish I had thought of that one myself. It is funny."

"Thank you," replied Ricky. "I like to write."

"Maybe you will be an author one day." Mr. Bennett took the briefcase from Ricky. He opened it. And he pulled out a brand-new copy of *Sloppy Sam*. Then he said, "Thank you again for finding my briefcase. I would be lost without it. I would like to give you something, Ricky."

Mr. Bennett opened *Sloppy Sam*. He took a pen out of his pocket. He wrote

something inside the book, and he gave the book to Ricky. Then he unlocked his car and climbed inside.

"Good-bye, Ricky," said Mr. Bennett.

"Good-bye." Ricky watched Mr. Bennett drive away. Then he looked inside the book. Mr. Bennett had written: *To Ricky, a future author and a great reader.*

And he had drawn a picture of a goose.

"Yes!" cried Ricky. He grinned. Then he snapped the book shut. And he ran back to Stoneybrook Academy to show it to the kids in Ms. Colman's class.

About the Author

ANN M. MARTIN lives in New York City and loves animals, especially cats. She has two cats of her own, Gussie and Woody.

Other books by Ann M. Martin that you might enjoy are *Stage Fright*; *Me and Katie (the Pest)*; and the books in *The Baby-sitters Club* series.

Ann likes ice cream and *I Love Lucy*. And she has her own little sister, whose name is Jane.

THE KIDS
IN
MS. COLMAN'S CLASS

A new series by Ann M. Martin

Don't miss #3
CLASS PLAY

On Thursday morning, Leslie felt butterflies in her stomach. As she walked down the hall to Ms. Colman's room, she leaned over and talked to her stomach.

"Go away, you butterflies," she said. "You are making me nervous. And I do not want to be nervous today."

"Who are you talking to?" asked Chris.

"No one," said Leslie. She felt her face turn red.

That morning Ms. Colman said to the kids in her class, "Remember, today is the day you will try out for parts in *Alice in Wonderland*. Mrs. Graff is going to meet us in the auditorium after lunch."

After lunch? thought Leslie. That is too bad. I am going to be very nervous by then. I hope I do not barf.